This book belongs to

This is the story of Gingerbread Fred.

You can read it in a chair, or read it in bed,

You can get someone else to read it instead!

There's something else. Can you guess what?

On every page there's a mouse to spot!

Text copyright © 2006 Nick and Claire Page

This edition copyright © 2011 make believe ideas ltd.

27 Castle Street, Berkhamsted, Herts, HP4 2DW. All rights reserved.

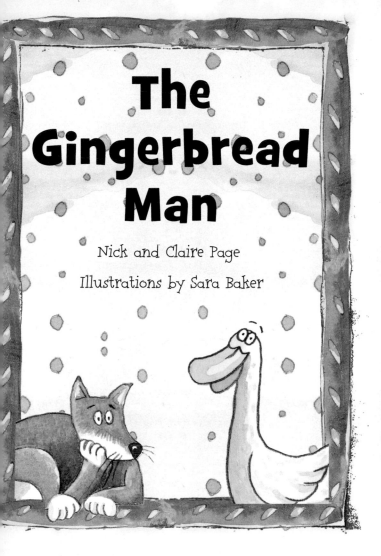

The Gingerbread Man

Nick and Claire Page

Illustrations by Sara Baker

make
believe
ideas

There once was a little old baker
and a little old baker's wife.
One day, they baked a gingerbread man,
who magically came to life!

The name that they gave him was
Gingerbread Fred.
And they said: "Don't go out on the street!
You are not a real boy, you're a biscuit –
and that makes you yummy to eat!"

But before you could say
"JELLY DOUGHNUTS,"
their gingerbread son
had started to run!

And Gingerbread Fred said . . .

"Run, run, run,
as fast as you can.
You can't catch me,
I'm the gingerbread man!"

First, Gingerbread Fred reached a garden,
where a cat lay asleep in the flowers.
"MEE-WOW!" said the cat.
"Here comes breakfast!
I've been waiting for hours and hours!"

But Fred didn't wait –
he started to skate!

And Gingerbread Fred said . . .

11

"Skate, skate, skate,
as fast as you can.
You can't catch me,
I'm the gingerbread man!"

Next, Gingerbread Fred reached a farmyard,
where a dog was lying about.

"BOW-WOW!" said the dog.

"It must be lunchtime!

It's a gingerbread man takeout!"

But before you could say,
"LEMON CHEESECAKE,"
Fred turned aside
and started to ride!

And Gingerbread Fred said . . .

"Ride, ride, ride,
as fast as you can.
You can't catch me,
I'm the gingerbread man!"

Then Gingerbread Fred reached the river,
where a fox sat, watching the fish.
"Need some help?" said the fox.
"Jump on my back.
I can take you across, if you wish."

Fred grabbed his coat
and the fox was a boat!

And Gingerbread Fred said . . .

"Swim, swim, swim,
as fast as you can.
You can't catch me,
I'm the gingerbread man!"

As the water gradually rose,
the fox said to Fred:
"Move up further.
It's best if you sit on my nose."

Quite soon, they were over the river,
and Gingerbread Fred said: "Good-bye!"
"Not so fast," said the fox.
"There's one more thing.
Now, how would you like to fly?"

And before you could say
"GINGER SNAPS,"
Fred was thrown high up in the sky!

And Gingerbread Fred said . . .

24

"Fly fly, fly,
as fast as you can.
You can't catch me,
I'm the . . ."

CRUNCH! SCRUNCH! MUNCH!
The fox had him for lunch.

And Gingerbread Fred
said nothing ever again.

Ready to tell

Oh no! Some of the pictures from this story have been mixed up! Can you retell the story and point to each picture in the correct order?

Picture dictionary

Encourage your child to read these words
from the story and gradually develop his
or her basic vocabulary.

baker

breakfast

fish

gingerbread
man

ride

river

run

skate

wife

Key words

Here are some key words used in context.
Help your child to use other words
from the border in simple sentences.

There **was** a little old baker.

They baked **a** gingerbread man.

"Fly as fast as you **can**."

The **dog** saw Gingerbread Fred.

"**Get** on my back."

Bake Gingerbread Fred

Ask a grown-up to help you bake Fred and his friends. You can eat them if they look like they're running away.

You will need

4 oz butter • 3 tbsp golden molasses • 1½ cups self-raising flour • ready-made icing in a tube • 1–2 tsp ground ginger • ½ cup superfine sugar • 1 egg, beaten • saucepan • mixing bowl • large spoon • greased baking sheet • a gingerbread-man cutter • colored chocolate beans

What to do

1 Turn the oven on to 350°F.

2 Melt the butter and molasses in a pan over a gentle heat.

3 Put the flour, ginger, and sugar in a mixing bowl. Add the melted butter and molasses, stir in slightly and then add the egg.

4 Mix the ingredients together until smooth and then leave for 15 minutes to cool.

5 Roll out to a thickness of ¼ inch and use the cutter to cut out the Gingerbread Fred shapes.

6 Place on the baking sheet and cook in the middle of the oven for about eight minutes, or until golden brown. Remove and leave to cool.

7 Decorate with icing eyes and mouth, and make buttons from colored chocolate beans stuck on with a spot of icing.